CATCHING THE SPEEDY THIEF

DINOSAUR COVE™

LATE CRETACEOUS

Attack of the
LIZARD KING

Charge of the
THREE-HORNED MONSTER

March of the
ARMOURED BEASTS

Flight of the
WINGED SERPENT

Catching the
SPEEDY THIEF

Stampede of the
GIANT REPTILES

JURASSIC

Rescuing the
PLATED LIZARD

Swimming with the
SEA MONSTER

Tracking the
GIGANTIC BEAST

Escape from the
FIERCE PREDATOR

Finding the
DECEPTIVE DINOSAUR

Assault of the
FRIENDLY FIENDS

TRIASSIC

Chasing the
TUNNELLING TRICKSTER

Clash of the
MONSTER CROCS

Rampage of the
HUNGRY GIANTS
COMING SOON

Haunting of the
GHOST RUNNERS
COMING SOON

Swarm of the
FANGED LIZARDS
COMING SOON

Snatched by the
DAWN THIEF
COMING SOON

DOUBLE LENGTH ADVENTURES

Journey to the
ICE AGE

Lost in the
JURASSIC
COMING SOON

DINOSAUR COVE™

CATCHING THE SPEEDY THIEF

by
REX STONE

illustrated by
MIKE SPOOR

Series created by
Working Partners Ltd

OXFORD
UNIVERSITY PRESS

Special thanks to Jane Clarke

For Guy Macdonald, a true explorer of adventures

OXFORD
UNIVERSITY PRESS

Great Clarendon Street, Oxford OX2 6DP
Oxford University Press is a department of the University of Oxford.
It furthers the University's objective of excellence in research, scholarship, and education by publishing worldwide in

Oxford New York

Auckland Cape Town Dar es Salaam Hong Kong Karachi
Kuala Lumpur Madrid Melbourne Mexico City Nairobi
New Delhi Shanghai Taipei Toronto

With offices in

Argentina Austria Brazil Chile Czech Republic France Greece
Guatemala Hungary Italy Japan Poland Portugal Singapore
South Korea Switzerland Thailand Turkey Ukraine Vietnam

Oxford is a registered trade mark of Oxford University Press in the UK and in certain other countries

Series created by Working Partners Ltd
Dinosaur Cove is a registered trademark of Working Partners Ltd

First published 2008
First published in this edition 2010

British Library Cataloguing in Publication Data

Data available

ISBN: 978-0-19-273170-8

1 3 5 7 9 10 8 6 4 2

Printed in Great Britain by Clays Ltd, St Ives plc
Paper used in the production of this book is a natural, recyclable product made from wood grown in sustainable forests
The manufacturing process conforms to the environmental regulations of the country of origin

FACT FILE

JAMIE HAS JUST MOVED FROM THE CITY TO LIVE IN THE LIGHTHOUSE IN DINOSAUR COVE. JAMIE'S DAD IS OPENING A DINOSAUR MUSEUM ON THE BOTTOM FLOOR OF THE LIGHT-HOUSE. WHEN JAMIE GOES HUNTING FOR FOSSILS IN THE CRUMBLING CLIFFS ON THE BEACH HE MEETS A LOCAL BOY, TOM, AND THE TWO DISCOVER AN AMAZING SECRET: A WORLD WITH REAL, LIVE DINOSAURS! THE BOYS HAVE EXPLORED THE JUNGLE, THE MARSH, AND THE CLIFFS, BUT WHEN THEY SPEND TIME AT THE LAGOON, THEY END UP FISHING FOR TROUBLE!

*NOTE: A JATOM IS THE SIZE OF JAMIE OR TOM: 125 CM TALL AND 27 KG IN WEIGHT

TOM

- **FULL NAME:** THOMAS CLAY
- **AGE:** 8 YEARS
- **SIZE:** 1 JATOM*
- **TOP SPEED:** 10 KPH
- **LIKES:** TRACKING ANIMALS AND EXPLORING WILDLIFE
- **DISLIKES:** RAINY DAYS

Tom's eye

Tom's hand

WANNA

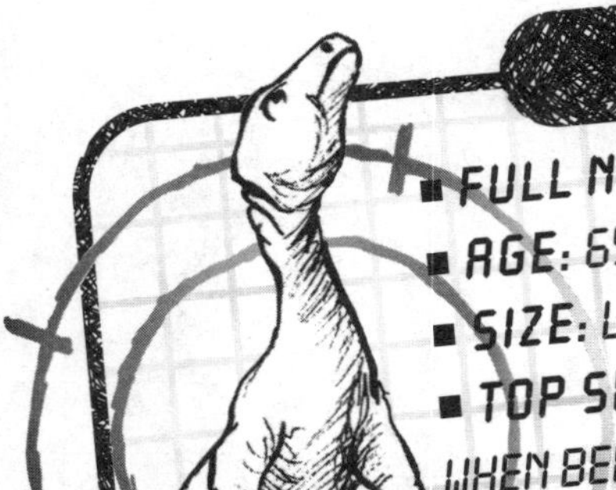

- **FULL NAME:** WANNANOSAURUS
- **AGE:** 65 - 80 MILLION YEARS**
- **SIZE:** LESS THAN A JATOM*
- **TOP SPEED:** 50 KPH, ESPECIALLY WHEN BEING CHASED BY A T-REX
- **LIKES:** STINKY GINGKO FRUIT AND BANGING HIS HEAD ON TREE TRUNKS
- **DISLIKES:** SCARY DINOSAURS

Wanna's head

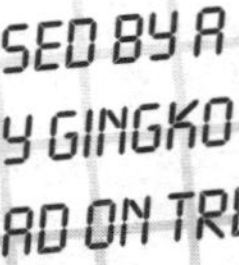

Wanna's foot

*__NOTE:__ A JATOM IS THE SIZE OF JAMIE OR TOM: 125 CM TALL AND 27 KG IN WEIGHT

**__NOTE:__ SCIENTISTS CALL THIS PERIOD THE LATE CRETACEOUS

VELOCIRAPTOR

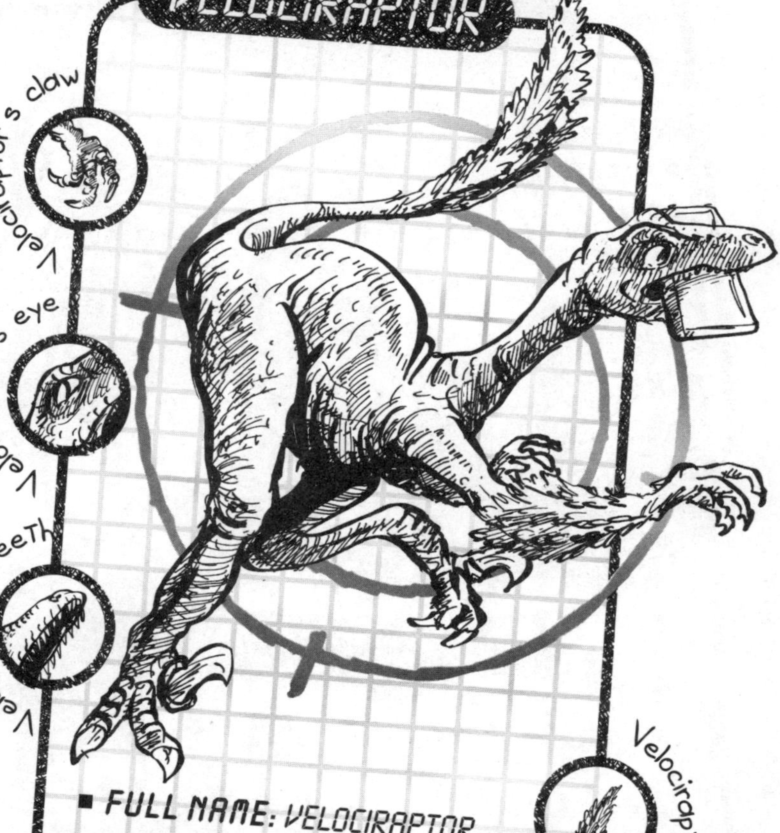

- **FULL NAME:** VELOCIRAPTOR
- **AGE:** 65 – 85 MILLION YEARS**
- **HEIGHT:** LESS THAN ONE JATOM*
- **LENGTH:** ONE AND A HALF JATOMS*
- **WEIGHT:** 1 JATOM*
- **TOP SPEED:** 56 KPH
- **LIKES:** PLAYING WITH HIS FOOD AND STEALING SHINY OBJECTS
- **DISLIKES:** THINGS THAT GET AWAY

***NOTE:** A JATOM IS THE SIZE OF JAMIE OR TOM: 125 CM TALL AND 27 KG IN WEIGHT
****NOTE:** SCIENTISTS CALL THIS PERIOD THE LATE CRETACEOUS

DINOSAUR COVE
Village
Marina
Sealight Head

Landslips where clay and fossils are
DINO CAVE
Muddy beach
igh Tide beach line
Low Tide beach line
Sea
Smuggler's Point

Jamie Morgan pulled a rainbow-coloured metal fish out of his grandad's tackle box and held it up for his friend Tom Clay to see. 'This fish has feathers!' A cluster of tiny pink and orange feathers sprouted out from where the tail should be.

'Different baits catch different beasts,' Jamie's grandad said with a grin, holding out his hand for the feathery fish. 'This spinner is great for catching sea bass. Now, let's see. What else will I need today?'

Fisherman's baits

sea bass spinner

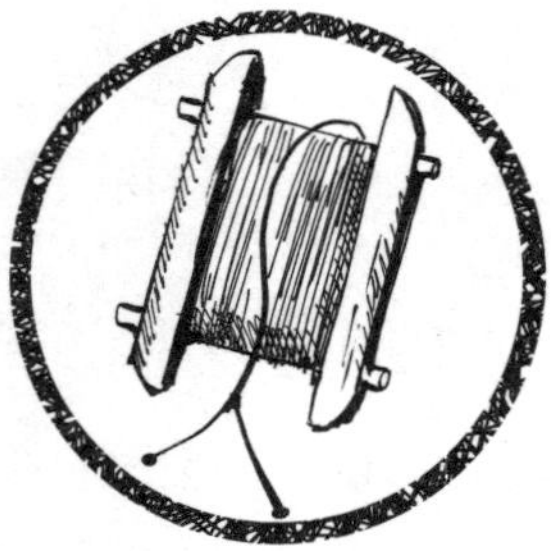

crab line

He tipped a tangle of weights, spinners, and fishing line onto the kitchen floor of the old lighthouse.

'What's this?' Jamie picked up an H-shaped piece of orange plastic with string wrapped around it and a couple of heavy lead weights dangling from it.

'Haven't you seen one before?' Tom said in amazement. 'It's a crab line.'

Jamie shook his head. 'How can this catch crabs?'

'It's easy,' Tom said. 'You tie a bit of bacon rind on the end and throw it in. The crabs grab the bacon and you grab the crabs!'

'Cool!' said Jamie. 'I'd like to try that.'

'The best place for crabbing is Sealight Head at high tide,' Grandad said, as he crammed everything but the crab line back in his tackle box. 'But high tide isn't until later this afternoon. I'll meet you there, if you like, after I've caught some sea bass for dinner.'

'OK, Grandad,' Jamie said as the old man finished packing his tackle box. 'We'll wait until then.'

'We don't have to wait,' Tom whispered to Jamie. 'We could go crabbing in Misty Lagoon in Dino World right now.'

Dino World was Jamie and Tom's secret—even Grandad didn't know that they'd found a world where real live dinosaurs lived.

'Great idea!' Jamie winked at Tom. 'We'll meet you near Sealight Head later, Grandad.'

'Don't forget the bait and mop bucket to put the crabs in,' Grandad told them. He pulled on his fishing boots. 'And I've put two cheese and pickle sandwiches in the fridge for you.'

He headed for the door. 'Have fun!'

'We will,' Tom said with a smile.

The minute Grandad was out of the door Tom grabbed the handle of the mop bucket. 'Got your Fossil Finder, Jamie?'

'Already in my backpack.' Jamie grinned as he wrapped two cheese and pickle sandwiches in shiny tinfoil and made a separate package for the bacon. He stuffed them in his backpack along with the crab line. 'Let's go!'

The boys clattered down the stairs of the lighthouse and dashed through the dinosaur exhibits on the ground floor. Jamie's dad was busy fixing a label to the wall next to the triceratops skull.

'How's the museum going, Mr Morgan?' Tom asked.

'Great, thanks,' said Jamie's dad. 'The Grand Opening is only a few days away.'

'See ya, Dad!' Jamie called, hurrying past the Late Cretaceous model and the T-Rex display. 'We're going crabbing.'

The boys scrambled down the rocky path from the lighthouse and ran along the beach onto the trail that led up Smuggler's Point. They bent double to catch their breath, and then clambered up the boulders to the smugglers' cave and squeezed through the gap at the back into the secret chamber.

'This is my favourite place in the whole world!' Jamie's heart began to pound as soon as he placed his feet into the fossilized dinosaur footprints on the cave floor.

'One . . . two . . . three . . . ' He counted each step. 'Keep close behind me, Tom.'

'You bet.' Tom's voice sounded excited. 'I wonder what we're going to find this time.'

'Four . . .'

A crack of light appeared in the cave wall in front of him.

'Five!' The ground squelched beneath Jamie's feet and he stood blinking in the bright sunshine and breathing in the familiar warm wet-leaf smell of Dino World.

A second later, Jamie and Tom were standing on Gingko Hill, and a rough, slobbery tongue was licking Jamie's hand.

'Ready for another adventure, Wanna?' Jamie asked their little dinosaur friend.

Jamie picked a stinky gingko fruit and held it out to the wannanosaurus.

Wanna took it gently, then greedily gobbled it up, wagging his tail and grunking as smelly gingko juice dribbled down his chin.

'It's almost like he was waiting for us,' Tom said with a laugh.

With Tom and Wanna close behind, Jamie strode through the trees to a curtain of creepers at the edge of Gingko Hill. As he pushed the creepers aside, excitement fizzed like soda in his stomach.

Beneath them lay the steamy emerald-green jungle. The air throbbed with the whirring and buzzing of insects, and the jungle rang with the strange calls of the weird and wonderful creatures that only lived in Dino World.

‘This has got to be the best place for adventures in the whole wide world!’ Jamie announced with a huge grin on his face.

‘In the whole solar system!’ Tom cheered.

‘In the whole universe!’ Jamie exclaimed.

Wanna grunked his agreement.

'Come on!' Jamie said. 'Let's see what we can catch in Misty Lagoon. We've only got until the tide comes in.'

The three friends clambered down the steep hillside into the dense jungle.

'We can follow the stream,' Jamie said, jumping into the shallow water that trickled and gurgled its way to the lagoon.

They splashed along the stream bed.

'That's where we met the T-Rex,' Tom said, pointing to a jumble of huge rounded rocks.

'I'll never forget those fangs.' Jamie shuddered. 'I hope he's not around today.'

'Me too,' said Tom, looking round nervously. 'Let's get a move on.'

They ran until they burst out of the jungle onto the palm-fringed sandy beach of the sparkling blue lagoon.

Jamie shaded his eyes with his hand and gazed round the shore. 'Which would be the best spot to find prehistoric crabs?'

'We need deep water for crabbing,' Tom told him. 'It's no use wading into the shallows.'

'How about over there?' Jamie pointed to an outcrop of fern-covered rocks on the north-east shore. A stone ledge stuck out of the ferns like a wide diving board, hanging over the deep, blue water.

'Perfect!' Tom declared.

Jamie led the way around the lagoon to the rocks and scrambled on top of them, pushing aside the

plants. It was an easy climb to the ledge over the water, and he put down his backpack in the shade of the tall ferns.

Tom scrambled up onto the ledge next to him. 'We can't see much through these ferns,' he said, glancing over his shoulder. 'But Wanna will warn us if anything tries to sneak up.'

He leaned over the lagoon and filled up the bucket with water. 'Time to bait the line.'

Jamie knelt on the rock ledge and dug inside his backpack.

'Here's the bacon.' Jamie handed Tom a tinfoil packet and then unravelled the crab line.

Wanna watched curiously as Tom unwrapped the bacon.

'No, Wanna, it's not for you,' Tom told the little dinosaur, tearing off the bacon rind. Wanna leaned over Tom's shoulder. His long tongue shot towards the bacon.

Gak gak gak!

Wanna spluttered in disgust. He spun around and grabbed a mouthful of fern leaves.

'He's trying to get rid of the taste,' Jamie said, tying the bacon rind onto the end of the line. 'Plant eaters don't eat bacon.'

Tom showed Jamie how to hold the orange plastic handle and carefully lower the crab line into the lagoon. Jamie felt the string run through his fingers until the weight came to rest on the bottom.

'Do I pull it up straight away?' he asked.

'No.' Tom laughed. 'You have to be patient. You'll feel a tug on the line when something takes the bait.'

'What if it isn't a crab?' Jamie asked. 'What if it's a huge electric eel?'

'Ooh,' Tom said. 'What if it's a humongous stingray?'

'What if it's a Loch Ness monster with ginormous fangs?' As Jamie laughed, a big bubble broke the mirror surface of the water.

Pop!

Jamie leapt to his feet, startling Wanna, who nearly fell backwards over the bucket.

But there was no giant creature leaping out at them. The lagoon was a calm mirror once more.

'False alarm,' Tom said. 'There's nothing there.'

Wanna started to chew a fern stem.

'Wanna's got the right idea,' Jamie said. 'Let's have lunch while we wait.'

'Good idea.' Tom rummaged in the backpack and pulled out the tinfoil packet. He took out a sandwich and handed it to Jamie.

'Your grandad's pickle is great!' Tom mumbled with his mouth full. 'Even if it does blow your head off,' he said between coughs.

'It is a bit spicy,' Jamie agreed, taking a huge bite. He felt a tug on the crab line. 'Something's taken the bait!' he spluttered, spraying a mouthful of crumbs all over the rock. He threw down his sandwich and

started to pull up the line as fast as he could. The line went limp.

Tom and Jamie peered over the ledge. 'It got away,' Jamie realized, as the end of the empty line came out of the water. 'It ate the bacon, too.'

'Better luck next time.' Tom tore off another strip of bacon and fixed it to the dripping line. Jamie threw it back in the water and reached for his sandwich.

'Where's my sandwich gone?' he said. There was a rustle in the ferns. Jamie whirled round in time to see the ferns stirring as a creature scurried away through them.

'Wanna!' Jamie yelled. 'You sandwich thief!'

Jamie gave the handle of the crab line to Tom and hopped off the rock into the ferns. He could hear a strange high-pitched rattling noise.

Ack ack ack!

'Wanna?' he called. 'Is that you?'

The ferns parted. The little dinosaur was bobbing his head and hopping excitedly

from foot to foot. His tongue was hanging out and he was making strange noises.

Jamie knew what that meant: Wanna must have been spluttering on Grandad's pickle. 'It's your own fault. You shouldn't have stolen my sandwich,' Jamie scolded him.

'Come quick!' Tom shouted from behind him. 'We've caught something

big!'

'One, two, three... heave!'

Jamie and Tom pulled on the crab line with all their might.

'Look at the size of that!' Tom gasped.

Dangling from the crab line was the biggest crab that Jamie had ever seen. Its shell was the size of a dinner plate. The crab's silvery shell shone in the sunshine as it held tight to the bacon on the end of the line. As Tom held the line, Jamie grabbed the bucket.

Wanna edged up and sniffed at the crab. It waved a pincer at him.

Grunk!

Wanna jumped back in alarm as Tom lowered the crab gently into the bucket.

'It's a good job this is a big bucket.' Jamie laughed.

They peered into the bucket. The crab was using its pincers to tear off small pieces of the bacon and shovel them into its mouth.

'Crabs haven't changed much since dino times,' Tom said thoughtfully.

Jamie took out his Fossil Finder and flipped it open. The '*HAPPY HUNTING*' screen popped up and he tapped *CRAB* into the search

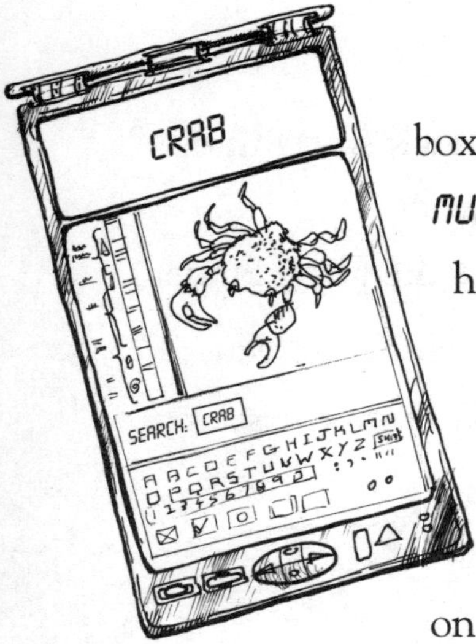

box. ' "*CRABS HAVEN'T CHANGED MUCH SINCE DINOSAUR TIMES*," ' he read aloud.

Tom laughed. 'That's what I said.'

Jamie snapped shut the Fossil Finder and put it on the rock beside him. 'I want to take a close look at this dino crab,' he told Tom. 'Help me get it off the line. It's wedged in the bucket, so it shouldn't nip us.'

Tom held the bucket steady and Jamie untangled the line from the crab's pincers.

Just when he had finished, there was a sudden rustle in the ferns behind them.

Ack ack ack!

Jamie spun round to see what was making the noise. A turkey-sized dinosaur with open toothy jaws dashed out from the plants onto the ledge beside them.

Tom almost dropped the bucket in surprise.

Snap!

The new dinosaur grabbed the Fossil Finder in its needle-sharp fangs.

Ack ack ack ack ack!

With a whip of the feathers on the end of its long yellow and orange tail, the two-legged dinosaur turned and darted into the ferns.

'What was that?' Tom said, still holding the bucket.

'Th-that . . . ' stammered Jamie, feeling the blood drain from his face, 'that was a velociraptor. A velociraptor just stole my Fossil Finder!'

Tom looked startled.

'We have to get it back,' Jamie said, shoving the crab line into his backpack.

Jamie crashed into the tall ferns and raced after the rapidly retreating raptor. Tom and Wanna plunged after him.

'It's heading towards the Far Away Mountains,' Tom said, as they emerged from the ferns into a section of the plains they hadn't been to before.

'Why did you bring the crab?' Jamie asked as they puffed along a shallow stream that flowed down to the lagoon.

Tom looked down in amazement at the

bucket that swung from his hand. 'Forgot I had it,' he said. 'I'll take it back later.'

Ahead of them, the velociraptor darted into a narrow passageway where the stream gushed between two huge rocks.

'Careful,' Tom said. 'We don't know what's on the other side of the rocks.'

'Time to find out.' Jamie stepped into the cool, fast-moving stream. Edging sideways like a crab, he squeezed through the narrow gap, followed closely by Tom and Wanna.

'Wow,' he breathed. 'It's like a rainbow!'

Ahead, the stream flowed through a rocky area streaked with splashes of bright orange, yellow, and green mud and cratered with deep blue pools that sparkled in the sunshine.

'There's the raptor!' Tom pointed to a reptilian tail disappearing into a cave on the other side of the pools.

'That must be where it lives.' Jamie heaved a sigh of relief. 'Urgh!' he sputtered. 'It stinks of rotten eggs around here.'

'Wanna likes it,' Tom said, glancing at the little dinosaur. Wanna was standing next to one of the small pools with his snout in the air, sniffing deeply.

'He would,' Jamie laughed. 'He likes anything stinky.'

Wanna cocked his head to one side and peered into the pool.

'Is he looking for more crabs?'

As Tom spoke, Wanna's pool burbled and bubbled. Pop! A wisp of hot steam escaped from a burst bubble and the smell of rotten eggs welled up.

'The water's hot,' Jamie chuckled. 'The only crabs he'll find in there will be bright pink cooked ones.'

Suddenly, there was a great

whoosh!

Wanna leapt back from the pool as a column of steaming water gushed high into the air.

Jamie watched it, mesmerized.

'Get out of the way!' Tom yelled as the column collapsed and a torrent of scalding water fell towards them.

Jamie, Tom, and Wanna dived behind a rock as scalding drops of water rained down.

'It's a geyser,' Tom said excitedly. 'I saw one on a TV programme about Yellowstone Park. The water's heated up by melted rock that bubbles up from the centre of the earth.'

The boys and Wanna peered out from behind the rock. On the other side of the pools, near the raptor's cave, there was a hissing and popping like a champagne cork and another geyser whooshed and spurted

into the air. Each of the six pools took their turn to shoot jets of hot water and steam into the air.

'No wonder that velociraptor's chosen to live in this cave,' murmured Tom. 'What other dinosaur would be fast enough to run past all the boiling geysers?'

'If we're careful, we can do it,' Jamie said. 'We've got to get the Fossil Finder back. If we leave it behind here, it might get fossilized—then someone in the future could dig up a computer next to a dinosaur fossil. We'll just have to learn the geysers' pattern.'

The boys watched as the geysers repeated their eruptions.

'I think I got it,' Jamie said.

The valley had gone quiet again. The only sound was the stream. It was as if nothing had happened.

'Now!' Tom yelled, clutching the crab bucket to his chest.

The boys and Wanna sprinted past the first pool.

Whoosh!

The huge geyser shot into the air behind them.

Whoosh!

'Watch out!' Jamie shouted. The three jumped into the stream and hid under an overhanging rock as the hot rain pattered into the water. As soon as it had passed, Wanna darted out and dashed past the second pool and the third, dodging the bubbling water.

'Follow Wanna!' Jamie yelled to Tom, and they raced after their dinosaur friend as all around them steaming fountains of scalding water exploded from mini-geysers.

In front of the cave, an aquamarine pool began to gurgle.

'Geyser about to blow!' Tom shouted above the sound of the fast-flowing stream. Jamie, Tom, and Wanna sprinted past the gurgling pool and hurled themselves behind a rock at the edge of the cave mouth as the last geyser exploded with a whoosh!

'That was close.'

Tom caught his breath and then peered into the bucket. 'The dino crab seems to be OK. It's waving its pincers, though. I think it's annoyed.'

'I'm not surprised.' Jamie grinned, glancing at his watch. 'We have to hurry,' he told Tom. 'It'll be high tide soon. We've got to get back before Grandad comes looking for us.'

'Sshh!' Tom whispered. 'Wanna can hear something.'

Wanna was peering into the cave with his tail sticking out stiffly behind him.

Ack ack ack ack ack!

A high-pitched rattle came from the back of the cave. Wanna shot backwards, making grunking noises.

'Hide!' Jamie hissed. The boys and Wanna ducked back behind the rock but nothing came out of the cave.

'We'll have to be careful,' Tom whispered, gently putting down the crab bucket. 'That's the raptor's den, and animals are dangerous if you corner them in their den.'

They peered into the cave. Against the wall, near the entrance, was a nest like a bird's, but woven from dried ferns, and the size of a car tyre. The sun was sparkling on shiny objects set among the brown stalks and leaves.

'Velociraptors must collect shiny things, like magpies,' Tom said. 'I can see the Fossil Finder!'

Jamie breathed a sigh of relief. 'It's really close and there's no sign of the raptor. He must have gone deeper into the cave. Maybe we can just grab the Fossil Finder and get out of here.'

Tom nodded. 'Let's try.'

They quietly crept into the gloomy, dank cave and tiptoed towards the velociraptor's nest. Jamie's foot crunched on something. *Ugh!* He looked down and shuddered. Well-gnawed bones were scattered around the huge nest.

'It's like the nest of a giant bird of prey,' Tom whispered from behind him. 'If that raptor gets us, we're in big trouble.'

A prickle of fear ran down Jamie's spine. He knew they had to be very careful.

Suddenly, the velociraptor shot out of the darkness, snarling viciously.

Ack ack ack ack ack!

Jamie threw himself backwards as the raptor pounced.

Snap!

The raptor's needle-sharp teeth closed on empty air.

'Get out, quick!' Tom grabbed Jamie by the T-shirt and pulled him out of the cave and back behind the rock, nearly knocking over the dino crab bucket in the process.

Once more, they peered around the rock with Wanna grunking softly behind them.

Ack ack ack ack ack!

The velociraptor was rattling softly to itself as it bent over its nest and carefully rearranged the position of the Fossil Finder in pride of place in the centre. The whoosh of the geysers exploded down the valley, drowning out all sound.

'If we lure it out of the cave,' Jamie whispered to Tom, 'then I can dash in and grab the Fossil Finder.'

'We lured the ankylosaurus out of the mud with flowers,' Tom said. 'But the velociraptor is a carnivore.'

Jamie glanced at the crab in the bucket. 'I've got an idea!' He rummaged in his backpack, took out the crab line and tied on the remains of the bacon.

'Cool!' Tom grinned, taking the line. 'I've never crabbed for dinosaurs before.'

Tom scrambled up onto the rocks above the cave and lowered the crab line so that the bacon dangled at raptor height in the mouth of the cave.

The valley quietened again as Jamie and Wanna flattened themselves behind the rock at the side of the cave entrance. Wanna grunked softly to himself.

'We have to be patient for crabbing,' Jamie told the little dinosaur.

Suddenly, the raptor lunged out of the mouth of the cave reaching for the bacon

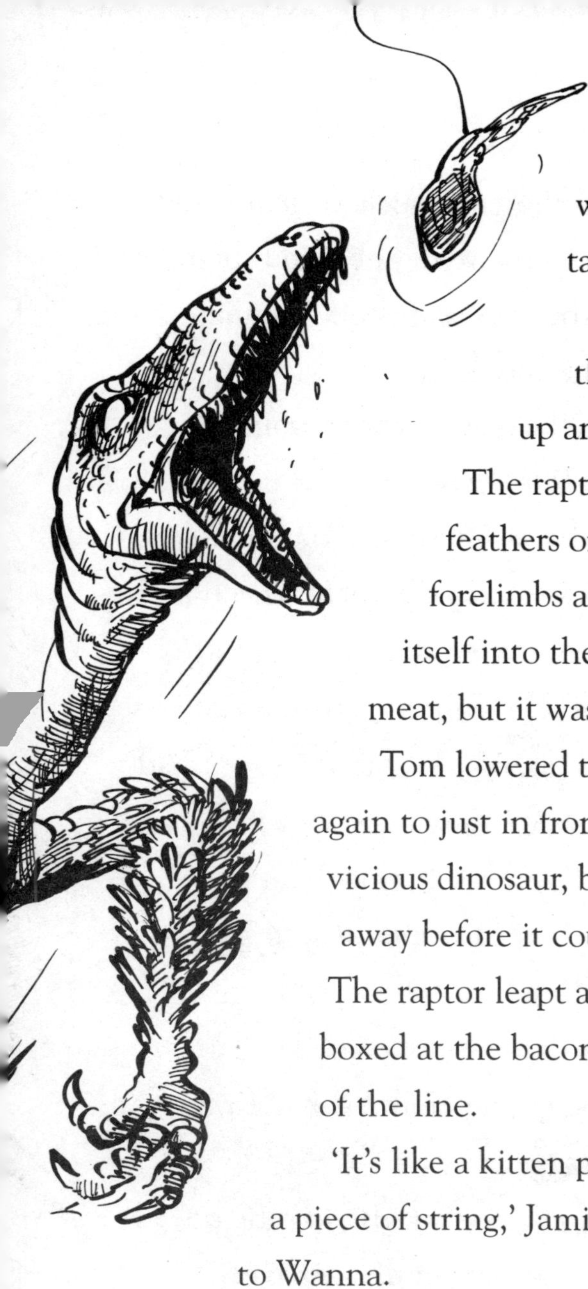

with its sharp talons, but Tom jerked the crab line up and away.

The raptor spread the feathers on its tail and forelimbs and launched itself into the air after the meat, but it was too high.

Tom lowered the bacon again to just in front of the vicious dinosaur, but pulled it away before it could grab it. The raptor leapt again and boxed at the bacon on the end of the line.

'It's like a kitten playing with a piece of string,' Jamie whispered to Wanna.

Tom edged along the rock shelf above the mouth of the cave, taking the bacon bait further and further away from where Jamie and Wanna were hiding.

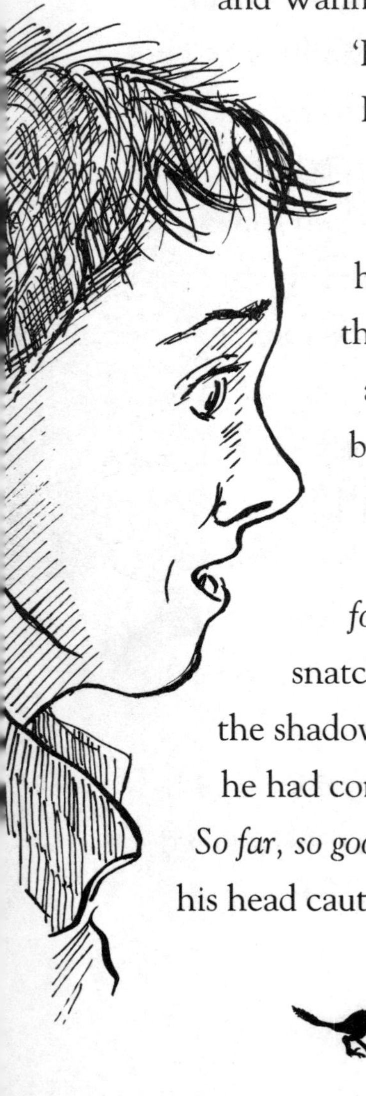

'It worked!' Jamie said.

He darted into the cave and grabbed the Fossil Finder out of the nest. He was about to hurry away when he spotted the foil that had been wrapped around his sandwich—it had been the raptor that stole his sandwich, not Wanna!

I can't leave that to get fossilized, he thought, snatching it up. Jamie kept to the shadows and crept back the way he had come.

So far, so good, he thought, and he poked his head cautiously out of the cave.

Instead of seeing Wanna's friendly face, two cold reptilian eyes stared unblinkingly back at him.

'Oh no!' Jamie breathed.

The velociraptor was back. It tilted its head to one side.

Ack ack ack!

The raptor rattled ominously and began to twitch its tail from side to side.

Ack
ack
ack!

Jamie's blood ran cold. It looked like a cat preparing to pounce on its prey.

'It's going to attack!' Tom screamed from the ledge above as the velociraptor spread its talon-like claws and came towards Jamie.

Jamie froze to the spot. Any moment now, the raptor's sharp teeth and claws would tear him to pieces.

Something scratched at the ground behind him. Jamie whirled round. Wanna! Wanna was revving up, getting a claw hold on the rock, his bony head lowered . . .

Gaaaaak!

The little dinosaur charged just as the velociraptor sprang at Jamie.

Thwack!

Wanna barged into the velociraptor and bowled it over.

As the raptor spat and rattled furiously, struggling to get back to its feet, Jamie and Wanna raced behind the rock.

'Mind the crab!' Jamie yelled. Too late. Wanna's tail smacked into the bucket and knocked it over. Jamie watched as the large dino crab tumbled out, pinched its claws at him, and scuttled away. It headed towards the stream, its silvery shell sparkling in the sunshine.

The stunned raptor stood up, shook itself, and looked around menacingly. Its tail feathers stiffened as it spotted the silvery crab scuttling past.

The raptor lunged after the crab. The crab darted this way and that as the raptor chased it.

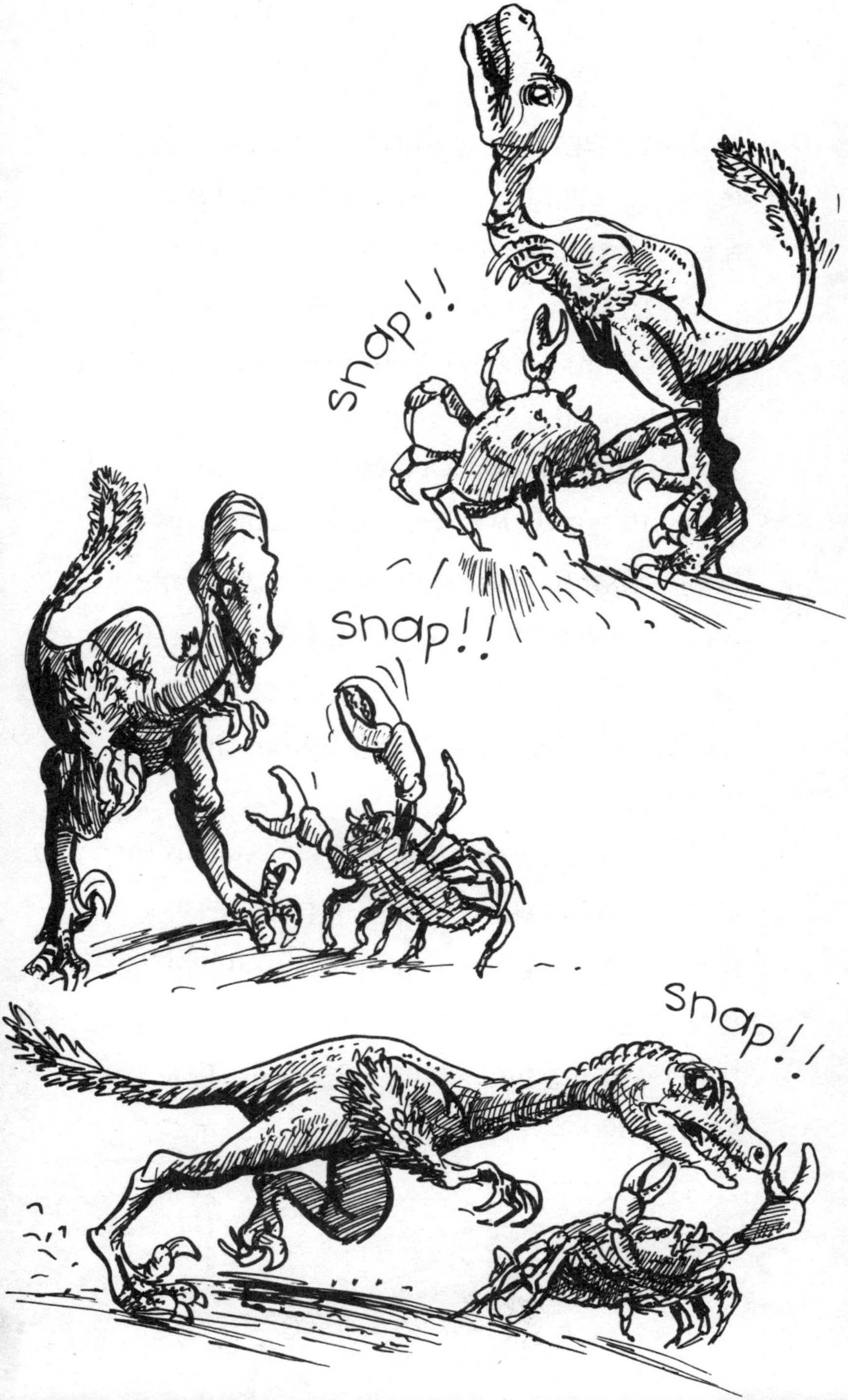
snap!!
snap!!
snap!!

'See! Raptors like shiny things!' Tom yelled from the ledge above the cave as the raptor turned, crouched and sprang towards the crab.

Snap!

The raptor's teeth crunched together on thin air.

Dino Crab hasn't got a chance, Jamie thought, but then stared in amazement as the crab waved its pincers defiantly at the raptor, rushed towards it, and pinched it on the calf of its left leg.

Ack! The raptor leapt back in surprise and pain.

'Go, Dino Crab!' the boys cheered, as the crab scuttled away from the raptor, towards the tumbling cool stream. They watched it plop into the water and sail like a boat downstream towards Misty Lagoon.

The velociraptor raced after the crab, dodging spouts of hot steam as one after another the geysers erupted all around it.

'Dino Crab can take care of itself.' Tom laughed. 'That velociraptor has met its match!'

Jamie looked at his watch. 'We better get back,' he yelled up to Tom.

'I can see Gingko Hill from up here,' Tom called down. 'We can go across the plains.'

'Great!' Jamie grabbed the bucket and he and Wanna clambered up onto the rock ledge above the cave. As they climbed, the green top of Gingko Hill rose in the distance. 'I'm glad we don't have to go back through the geysers.'

Wanna greeted Tom with a wag of his tail, then strode off along the narrow path that led away from the cave. At the top, Jamie put down the bucket and shaded his eyes to look

out across the gently rolling plains that lay between them and Gingko Hill. On the edge of the plains, a herd of small stocky dinosaurs with big bony neck frills and parrot-like beaks was grazing peacefully on the horsetail ferns.

Jamie rummaged in his backpack and took out the Fossil Finder. Its shiny case was dented with raptor tooth marks. He rubbed off a streak of dried raptor dribble and then flipped it open.

'It still works,' he said in relief as he typed in '*NECK FRILL*' and '*BEAK*' .

Tom looked over his shoulder. '*PROTOCERATOPS.*' he read. 'They're harmless.' He put the crab line in the bucket and picked it up. 'And they wouldn't be browsing if any carnivores were around.'

Wanna bobbed his head as if in agreement, turned, and set off towards Gingko Hill followed by Tom. Jamie snapped the Fossil Finder shut, crammed it into his backpack, and hurried after them.

'He knows all the paths around here,' Tom said as Wanna confidently led them past the herd of peaceful protoceratops and through the jumbles of rock and tangles of tree ferns that littered the plains. They followed the little dinosaur across the stream and back up the conifer-carpeted hillside to the top of Gingko Hill.

Jamie checked his watch. 'We should make it in time to meet Grandad,' he said, giving Wanna a pat on the head. 'Bye, Wanna, see you next time. Sorry I accused you of stealing my sandwich.'

Jamie picked a handful of gingko fruit and the little dinosaur grunked happily as he settled down by his nest and began to munch on the stinky fruit.

Tom looked at his watch. 'We'll have to hurry,' he announced.

The boys carefully placed their feet in the fresh dinosaur prints outside the rock face and stepped backwards out of the bright sunshine of Dino World into the darkness of the smugglers' cave. They squeezed through the gap, dashed out of the cave, and burst out onto Smuggler's Point. Beneath them the waves were swirling close to the rocks.

'The beach will be cut off any minute,' Tom said. 'It's almost high tide.'

They sprinted down the path and reached the beach just as the first gentle waves lapped at the bottom of the pathway.

'Just in time!' Jamie shouted, as they splashed through the shallow water and hurried to the other side of the cove.

'Ahoy there, me hearties!' Grandad greeted them with a wave from the rocks beneath Sealight Head. 'Are you ready for a crabbing adventure?'

'Just as long as there are no geysers or raptors,' Tom whispered to Jamie as they scrambled up the rocks to join him.

Jamie grinned. 'Ahoy there, Grandad,' he called. 'We're always ready for a new adventure!'

DINOSAUR WORLD
BOYS' ROUTE
Jungle
Misty Lagoon
White Ocean

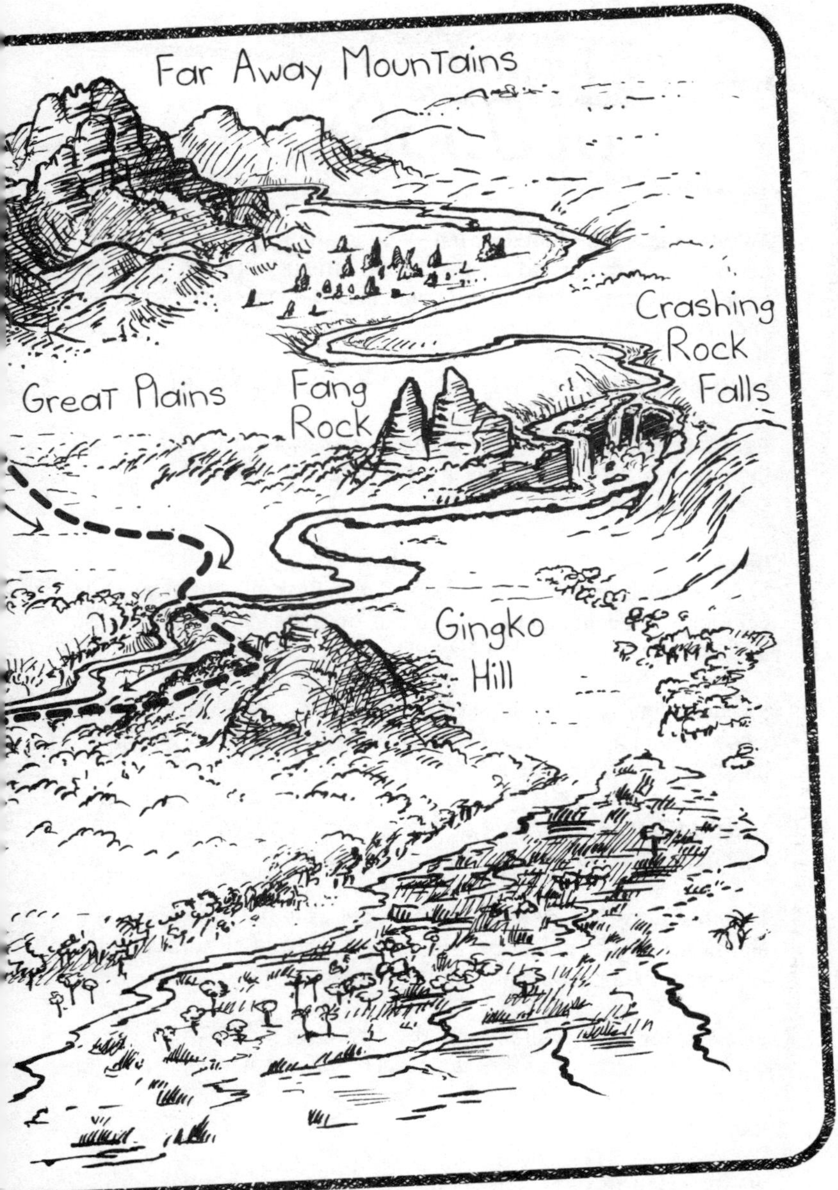
Far Away Mountains
Crashing Rock Falls
Great Plains
Fang Rock
Gingko Hill

GLOSSARY

Ankylosaurus (an-ki-low-sor-us) – a vegetarian dinosaur known for its armoured coat and clubbed tail. Its armour consisted of large bony bumps similar to the covering of modern-day crocodiles and lizards.

Fossil Finder – hand-held computer filled with dinosaur facts.

Geyser (gee-ser) – a hot spring, heated by volcanic activity below the earth's surface, that erupts in a tall stream of hot water and steam from time to time.

Gingko (gink-oh) – a tree native to China called a 'living fossil' because fossils of it have been found dating back millions of years, yet they are still around today. Also known as the stink bomb tree because of its smelly apricot-like fruit.

Protoceratops (pro-toe-serra-tops) – a horned, plant-eating dinosaur with a large head, neck frill and parrot-like beak, roughly half the size of a triceratops.

Triceratops (T-tops) (try-serra-tops) – a three-horned, plant-eating dinosaur which looks like a rhinoceros.

Tyrannosaurus Rex (T-Rex) (ti-ran-oh-sor-us rex) – a meat-eating dinosaur with a huge tail, two strong legs but two tiny arms. T-Rex was one of the biggest, scariest dinosaurs.

Velociraptor (ve-loss-i-rap-tor) – meat-eating dinosaur which was one of the smartest and fastest dinosaurs. Velociraptors were about the size of a turkey with a large curved claw on both of its feet.

Wannanosaurus (wah-nan-oh-sor-us) – a dinosaur that only ate plants and used its hard, flat skull to defend itself. Named after the place it was discovered: Wannano in China.

Get out of my way!

I'm charging in soon . . .